DISNEY'S

MULAN

Adapted by Cathy East Dubowski

DISNEY PRESS

New York

Adapted from
Walt Disney Pictures' MULAN
Music by MATTHEW WILDER Lyrics by DAVID ZIPPEL
Original score by JERRY GOLDSMITH
Produced by PAM COATS
Directed by BARRY COOK and TONY BANCROFT

Printed in the United States of America

First Edition
1 3 5 7 9 10 8 6 4 2

The text for this book is set in 14-point Hiroshige.

Library of Congress Catalog Card Number: 97-80190

ISBN: 0-7868-4222-9

For more Disney Press fun, visit www.DisneyBooks.com

Prologue

For thousands of years, life was good in the land of China. The people worked hard, tilling the soil, and reaped the gifts of the good earth.

But then one day barbaric Huns attacked from the north. They destroyed villages and burned temples. The people lived in fear.

The emperor ordered a great wall to be built along the Chinese border to keep out the enemy and protect his people.

Years passed. Each new emperor added to the wall, stone by stone, for hundreds of years. At last the Great Wall of China wove through the mountains like a dragon.

And for a long time there was peace.

But then one day a bloodthirsty new warrior rose up to lead the Huns. His name was Shan-Yu. And even the Great Wall could not keep him out.

General Li, leader of the Imperial Army, hurried to the throne room to tell the emperor the news. The Huns had crossed the border.

"We'll set up defenses around your palace immediately," General Li assured the emperor.

"No," the concerned ruler replied. "Send your troops to defend my people, Chi Fu!" the emperor called to his chief aide.

Chi Fu stood at attention. "Yes, Your Majesty."

"Deliver army papers throughout the land," the emperor commanded. "Call up reserves and as many new recruits as possible. I will not take any chances. A single grain of rice can tip the scale."

He gazed out the window at the land he loved.

"One man may be the difference between victory and defeat."

Chapter One

In a small Chinese village a young woman named Fa Mulan bent over a scroll. She was studying for a test.

How can they possibly expect me to remember all this? she wondered with a frown.

Then she had an idea. She dipped her brush into a pot of black ink. As she read, she copied the words onto her arm—words that told her how to be the perfect Chinese woman.

"She must be quiet, graceful, polite," she wrote. She stopped to use chopsticks to shove another hearty bite of rice into her mouth. Mumbling over the food, she went on, "Refined, poised, always on time . . ."

Cock-a-doodle-doooo!

Mulan's eyes flew to the window. "Aii-ya! I'm late!" she cried. And she still hadn't fed the chickens!

Mulan scrambled to her feet. She couldn't be late—today of all days! She needed help—and fast. "Little Brother!" she called out, running through the house. "Little Brother—"

There he was, lying on the ground—her adorable little dog! "Who's the smartest doggy in the world? Come on, smart boy."

Mulan tied a small bag of chicken feed to her dog's tail. Next she tied a bone to a stick. Then she hooked that to her dog's collar so the bone dangled over the dog's head. Grinning, she opened the door.

Zip! The dog dashed into the yard, chasing the bone that danced inches beyond his nose. As he ran, the sack of chicken feed spilled across the yard. The chickens clucked and squawked as they pecked up the grain.

Maybe that's the way to feed the chickens every morning! Mulan thought, proud of herself. Smiling, she ran to fix her father's morning tea.

Mulan's father, Fa Zhou, walked stiffly into the family temple. First he lit some smoky incense. Then he used his cane to lower himself carefully to his knees before the stone tablets of his ancestors. He was not that old a man. But some days the old war wound in his leg made him feel positively ancient.

Fa Zhou often prayed to his ancestors about important matters. But today he had only one thought on his mind. His daughter, Mulan. His greatest joy—and his greatest concern!

She was not like most young girls. She would rather dash over the hills on that horse of hers than dress up demurely. She spoke her mind even though it was a woman's place to be unheard and unseen. A smile tugged at Fa Zhou's lips. And smart! Mulan was always thinking up new ways to do things.

He feared his wife found little joy or humor in Mulan's behavior. Fa Li tried to raise her daughter in the ancient traditions, as she herself had been raised.

Fa Zhou sighed. He knew there was but one path for a young girl in China. One way to bring honor to herself and to her family.

First, she must please the matchmaker, who would find her a good husband so that she could become an obedient wife and daughter-in-law. And to do that she must be ladylike, graceful, quiet . . .

Fa Zhou sighed and bowed his head again. He had his work cut out for him! "Honorable ancestors," he prayed, "please help Mulan impress the matchmaker today. She—"

Mulan's dog, Little Brother, burst into the sacred temple with a bone dangling over his head.

Bwaak! Bwaak! Bwaak!

Seconds later feathers flew as a flock of chickens ran in after him.

Fa Zhou sighed. He knew this was Mulan's doing. He bent his head to pray some more.

His unusual daughter needed all the help she could get.

Mulan hurried.

But not to the matchmaker's. She was hurrying to the temple to take her father his morning tea.

"Father," she called out, "I brought you your—"

Crash! She ran into her father just as he stepped from the temple. Fa Zhou managed to catch the teapot with the crook of his cane. But the teacup crashed to the steps.

"Don't worry," Mulan said, well aware of her shortcomings. "I brought a spare."

"Mulan—," her father began.

"Remember," Mulan said as she poured the steaming tea into the delicate cup, "the doctor said three cups of tea in the morning."

"Mulan—"

"And three at night," she went on.

"Mulan!" her father exclaimed. "You should already be in town. There are no second chances with the matchmaker. We're counting on you to uphold the family honor."

Mulan flashed him a reassuring grin. "Don't worry, Father. I won't let you down." She held her arm behind her back so he couldn't see the cheat sheet she'd written on it. "Wish me luck!"

11

"Hurry!" her father called as she ran for her horse. He turned and went back into the temple. Just in case, he'd better pray some more!

Mulan's mother waited in the village. She stared down the busy street, while carts and rickshas whizzed past. Where was Mulan?

"I should have prayed to the ancestors for luck!" Fa Li anxiously said to Grandmother Fa.

The old woman shook her head. "How lucky can they be? They're dead!" But then she held up something. A present she had just bought for Mulan in the marketplace.

A tiny cricket in a small bamboo cage.

Crickets were known to be good luck, and Grandmother Fa believed in good luck charms.

But first Grandmother Fa decided to test this cricket's luck. She covered her eyes, held out the cage, and walked straight into the middle of the busy street!

Carts and rickshas crashed into one another as they swerved to avoid the old woman. Miraculously she made it safely to the other side.

Grandmother Fa called out in delight, "Yep! This cricket's a lucky one!" Inside the cage, the little cricket fainted.

Chapter Two

"Fa Li," the village bather said impatiently. "Is your daughter here yet?"

Fa Li put on the pleasant smile she'd been taught to wear even when she was not smiling inside. "I am sure Mulan will be here soon."

Soon Mulan was racing toward the village on the back of her horse, Khan. How she loved the rhythm of the galloping horse! The wind whistling past her ears made her feel wild and free. At last Khan slowed to a halt. As the dust settled, she jumped from the horse and hurried toward her mother. "I'm here!"

Fa Li frowned at her daughter. The girl was a complete mess! She was covered in dust and her hair was tangled with leaves and twigs.

Mulan's smile faded as she looked at her mother's exasperated expression. "What?"

Fa Li said not a word, but grabbed her daughter by the hand and marched her to the bather's shop.

"But, Mama, I had to—"

"None of your excuses!" her mother said sternly. "Let's get you bathed."

Soon Mulan sat shivering in a tub full of soapy water. Her mother and the village bather began to scrub her from head to toe. "It's freezing!" she wailed.

"It would've been warm if you'd been here on time," her mother pointed out. As she began to scrub her arm, she stopped and stared. "Mulan! What's this?"

"Notes," Mulan muttered. "In case I forget something?"

Fa Li rolled her eyes heavenward and prayed. Grandmother Fa headed out to the village shops. "We'll need more luck than I thought."

Next, Mulan's mother hurried her into the hairdresser's shop. Two women pulled and yanked her long black hair as they fought the tangles into a respectable hairdo.

At the dressmaker's they stuffed Mulan into a beautiful silk dress. But they pulled it so tight, she could hardly breathe!

At the makeup shop her eyes were lined to make them dark and mysterious. Her face was dusted with white rice powder. Red rouge was rubbed into her cheeks and lips.

When they were finished, Mulan gazed into the mirror.

Who is that girl? she thought. She was lovely—but a total stranger.

Mulan took a tiny piece of hair and

curled it over her forehead. There—that was a little better.

Fa Li unwrapped a piece of cloth. Inside lay a beautiful decorative comb. Smiling happily, she tucked it in her daughter's hair. "There, my daughter. Now you are ready."

Mulan sighed. She wanted more than anything to please her mother and father. And to bring honor to the family. If this was what it took—a little makeup, uncomfortable clothes—well, she could bear it if it made them happy.

Grandmother Fa pushed in between them. "Not yet!" She had more gifts for Mulan—gifts of tradition that must not be forgotten. An apple for serenity. A pendant for balance. And beads of jade for beauty. Then she tied the tiny bamboo cage to Mulan's waist. "And a cricket for good luck." At last—Mulan was ready to meet the matchmaker!

Mulan gulped as she joined the other young women in front of the matchmaker's house.

The time had come. Her entire future—and her family's honor—rested on her success with the matchmaker.

"Ancestors," she prayed as she waited, "help me not make a fool of myself."

"Fa Mulan!"

Mulan looked up eagerly into the face of the matchmaker and waved her hand. "Present!" she shouted loud and clear.

The matchmaker frowned and scribbled on her tablet. "Speaking without permission . . ."

Ooops!

Mulan followed the matchmaker into her house. The matchmaker circled her and looked her up and down. Mulan felt as if she were a horse to be bought and sold.

The matchmaker clucked her tongue. "Too

skinny. Hmmph! Not good for bearing sons."

As she wrote more notes, Cri-Kee escaped from his cage and hopped onto the matchmaker's shoulder!

Yikes! That was all she needed! Mulan picked off the tiny cricket just as the matchmaker turned around.

Without thinking, Mulan popped the cricket into her mouth to hide it. Still she smiled. Now that was *poise*!

"Recite the Final Admonition," the matchmaker ordered.

The moment of truth, and Mulan was caught with a mouthful of cricket!

"Well?" the matchmaker demanded.

Mulan flicked open her fan to hide her face and spat the cricket into the palm of her hand. Then she began to recite. "Fulfill your duties calmly and . . . uh . . ."

Thank goodness she'd made those notes on her arm! She pushed up her sleeve and stole a peek.

Oh no—the bath had smeared the ink! She squinted at the words, trying to read. "Uh, respectfully. . . . Reflect before you snack—uh, act!"

The matchmaker stared at her suspiciously.

"This shall bring you honor and glory," Mulan concluded. Whew!

Suddenly the matchmaker snatched the fan. The girl must be cheating! But she found nothing. Scowling, she grabbed Mulan's arm and led her to a small table. "Now pour the tea."

Mulan nearly gasped. The ink on her arm had rubbed off on the matchmaker's hand.

Nervously Mulan knelt.

"To please your future in-laws," the matchmaker said, "you must demonstrate a sense of dignity and refinement."

The old woman stroked her face imperiously—and left an inky black mustache.

Mulan gawked—and accidentally poured the tea onto the table. She quickly recovered and poured tea into the matchmaker's cup, but panicked when she noticed the little cricket relaxing in the tea.

The matchmaker went on, "You must also be poised—"

"Umm, pardon me," Mulan began.

"And *silent!*" The matchmaker glared at Mulan, then raised the cricket-filled teacup toward her lips.

"Ummm, could I just take that back—for a moment?" Mulan asked nervously. She grabbed the cup and pulled.

Splash! Tea spilled down the front of the matchmaker's dress—along with the tiny cricket!

The matchmaker screamed and jumped to her feet. "Why, you clumsy—"

Crash! The matchmaker knocked over the incense burner and landed in the hot coals. Mulan tried to help. She fanned at the matchmaker's backside, trying to cool the heat.

Whoosh! The matchmaker's hot clothes burst into flames. Mulan ran into the streets, carrying the teapot.

The matchmaker shoved past her, screaming, "Put it out! Put it out!"

Mulan yanked off the teapot lid and threw tea at the flames. The liquid put out the fire. But the matchmaker was soaked.

And her face was steaming.

Mulan's cheeks burned with shame as curious villagers gathered in the street to whisper and stare.

"You are a *disgrace!*" the matchmaker shouted, loud enough for all to hear. "You may look like a bride—but you will *never* bring your family honor!"

Chapter Three

Mulan's feet dragged as she led Khan home and through the front gate.

Her father was waiting for her, smiling hopefully.

Mulan gulped. She *couldn't* face him! She couldn't bear to see the shame and disappointment in his eyes when he learned of her failure. She hid behind Khan as she led him to the stable. As Khan drank from his trough, Mulan stared at her reflection in the water.

She had tried to play the part of the perfect bride and the perfect daughter, but she had failed again and again. "If I were truly to be myself, I'd break my family's heart."

Mulan wandered into the garden and sat down on a bench beneath a tree heavy with pink blossoms. Thinking of her mother's shame, she removed the beautiful comb from her hair.

Behind her someone cleared his throat.

Father! Surely by now he must be aware of her disgraceful failure.

Mulan knew she deserved a scolding. She bowed her head obediently, waiting for her father to speak.

Fa Zhou sat down beside her. He took his time, as if searching for the perfect words. But when he spoke, his voice held no anger. "What beautiful blossoms we have this year," he said, staring into the tree above them. "But look."

His hand touched a blossom that had yet to open.

"This one is late," he said softly. He took the comb from Mulan's hands and tucked it into her hair. "But I'll bet that when it

blooms, it will be the most beautiful of all."
Mulan could hardly believe it. Her father was not angry! She smiled at him. His gentle words soothed her.

Suddenly a sound like thunder rumbled through the garden. Fa Zhou rose to his feet and leaned heavily upon his cane. A frown creased his brow.

Together, they joined Fa Li and Grandmother Fa at the front gate. A villager was pounding a huge drum as soldiers galloped into town.

"Mulan," her mother called sharply. "Stay inside."

Behind them, Grandmother Fa winked and motioned toward the wall. Quickly Mulan scrambled up so she could see.

"Citizens!" cried Chi Fu, the emperor's aide. "I bring a proclamation from the Imperial City! The Huns have invaded China!"

The crowd gasped. This was frightening news indeed!

The man held up the proclamation and read: "By order of the emperor, one man from every family must serve in the Imperial Army." Then he began to call out the names.

"The Hsiao family!"

A middle-aged man came forward to take his papers.

"The Yi family!"

Mulan saw a bent old man step from the crowd, along with his tall, strong-looking young son.

"I will serve the emperor in my father's place," the young man declared.

"The Fa family!"

A chill ran down Mulan's spine. "No!" she whispered.

The crowd murmured. Everyone knew of Fa Zhou's past service in the emperor's army. And they knew of his injury.

Mulan's father handed his cane to his wife. Then, gathering his strength, he proudly stepped forward. "I am ready to serve the emperor."

Mulan jumped from the wall and ran into the street. "Father!" she cried. "You cannot go!"

"Mulan!" her father said, his voice full of warning.

"Please, sir," she begged the soldier. "My father has already fought bravely for the emperor—"

"Silence!" Chi Fu bellowed. He glared at Fa Zhou. "You would do well to teach your daughter to hold her tongue in a man's presence."

Mulan winced at the look of shame on her father's face.

"Mulan," he said curtly, "you dishonor me."

She felt a hand on her arm as Grandmother Fa led her away. Behind her she heard Chi Fu tell her father, "Report tomorrow to the Wu Zhong camp."

"Yes, sir," Fa Zhou replied. Then he walked proudly past his wife. With the eyes of the villagers and soldiers upon him, he refused to take his cane.

Chi Fu called out other names. But Mulan heard none of them. Only one name mattered to her: her father's.

Later that day, Mulan peeked into her father's room. Fa Zhou stood before the cabinet that held his armor.

He took out his magnificent sword. With great skill he sliced the shining blade through the air, as if challenging Shan-Yu himself in battle.

Suddenly he gasped, grasping his leg in pain. The sword clattered to the floor as he crumpled to his knees.

Slowly, painfully, he pulled himself to his feet.

Mulan pressed herself against the wall so her father would not see her. Her heart pounded as she faced the truth. If her father went to war, she knew he would never return.

That night at dinner Mulan could barely eat. Her father, mother, and grandmother ate in silence.

How can they be so calm! Mulan thought angrily. This could be our last night together—forever!

At last she could hold it in no longer. She slammed down her cup, splashing tea onto the table. "You shouldn't have to go!" she cried.

"Mulan . . . ," her mother cautioned.

But Mulan ignored her mother's warning and jumped to her feet. "There are plenty of young men to fight for China!"

Fa Zhou looked up from his rice bowl and said calmly, "It is an honor to protect my country—and my family."

"So you'll die for honor!?" Mulan challenged.

"I will die doing what's right!"

"But if you—"

"I know my place!" her father bellowed. Then his voice grew quiet and stern. "It is time *you* learned *yours*."

Tears stung Mulan's eyes. How could he speak to her that way? Didn't he understand her concern for him? Without another word, she ran from the table and out into the night. There, all alone, she let her tears fall.

Chapter Four

Mulan sat at the foot of the Great Stone Dragon that stood in the middle of her family's garden. With a troubled mind she stared at her reflection in a puddle.

Lightning streaked across the sky. Thunder roared, startling her from her thoughts. Across the garden a light glowed from her parents' window. She could see her father's silhouette as he tried to comfort her mother. But her mother only pulled away.

Moments later her father blew out the candle, plunging the room into darkness. Mulan ignored the raindrops that soaked her hair and spilled down her face. For she had come to a decision. She knew what she must do.

Mulan splashed through the puddles as she ran for the temple. Inside she lit a stick of incense and placed it in a tiny dragon incense holder.

She did not know that someone watched her as she said a quick prayer: the tiny good-luck cricket that her grandmother had given her that morning. When she scrambled to her feet and hurried out, Cri-Kee hopped after her.

Dripping wet, Mulan slipped into the house. Thunder and lightning hid the sound of her footsteps as she tiptoed to her parents' room.

Good. They were asleep.

As silent as a shadow she stole into their room. With trembling fingers, she slid her father's army paper from the table beside their bed. In its place, she left the beautiful comb from her hair. She gazed at her father tenderly for a moment, then fled from the room.

Alone in the front room she held up her father's sword.

For a moment she hesitated. The thing she was about to do could not be undone. But do it she must.

Whack! With one flash of the blade she sliced off her long black hair.

Out in the stables, Khan whinnied in alarm.

A warrior stood in the shadows.

But then the figure stepped forward. Mulan—dressed in her father's armor—reached out to calm her horse.

She had chosen her path—a road very different from the one her parents wished for her.

She would pretend to be her father's son. She would fight in his place to save his life.

Mulan knew the danger well. It was

against Chinese law for a female to be a soldier. The penalty: certain death. But her heart told her, Go! Go on!

And so she leaped onto Khan and galloped out the front gate.

Boom! Grandmother Fa bolted upright in bed, her eyes wide.

Something was wrong!

Her slippers slapped the floor as she hurried through the darkened house. Checking here, checking there. And then she burst into her son's room. "Mulan is gone!"

Mulan's parents sat up in alarm.

Fa Zhou's eyes fell upon the nightstand. He picked up Mulan's comb with trembling fingers. "It can't be . . ." He ran to his closet. His armor and sword were gone, too! He rushed into the rainy courtyard. "Mulan!" he wailed.

But his only answer was the banging

34

of the front gate in the pouring rain.

His daughter was gone! And there was no doubt in his mind what she intended to do.

Fa Li rushed to her husband's side. "You must go after her! She could be killed!"

"If I *reveal* her," Fa Zhou replied, "she *will* be."

Grandmother Fa pleaded, "Ancestors, hear our prayer. Watch over Mulan."

Chapter Five

Wind gusted into the Fa family temple, blowing out the candles and the incense Mulan had left burning. In the darkness, the spirit of the First Ancestor appeared.

"Mushu!" he shouted at the dragon incense burner. "Awaken!"

The incense burner trembled. And then, from the thick smoke curling around it, a living dragon appeared.

A minidragon.

"I live!" he crowed. He rubbed his hands together, ready to go to work. "So, tell me what mortal needs my protection, great ancestor. You just say the word, and I'm there!"

The First Ancestor rolled his eyes. Then he pointed at the stone animals that lined the room. "*These* are the family guardians. And they . . . ?"

Mushu shrugged. "Protect the family."

"And you, O *demoted* one . . . ?"

Mushu hung his head. "Ring the gong."

The First Ancestor nodded. "Now wake up the ancestors!"

Mushu sighed. "One family reunion coming right up," he muttered. Then he picked up his stick and began to wham the daylights out of the gong. "Okay, people! Look alive! Rise and shine! You're all way past the beauty sleep thing. Trust me!"

Slowly the room filled with the spirits of the Fa ancestors.

"I knew it!" one complained right away. "That Mulan was a troublemaker from the start!"

"Don't look at me," the one beside her

replied. "She gets it from your side of the family."

"She's just trying to help her father," another protested.

"But if she's discovered," another put in, "Fa Zhou will be forever shamed. Dishonor will come to the family."

"My children never caused such trouble," one said smugly.

"Let a guardian bring her back!" another cried.

An excited murmur swept through the room.

The First Ancestor nodded. "We must send the most powerful of all."

Mushu the little dragon stood up proud and tall. "I'll go!"

Laughter shook the temple.

"You had your chance to protect the Fa family," an ancestor scolded. "Your mistake led Fa Dang to disaster."

Across the room the spirit of Fa Dang

held his head in his hand. "Yeah, thanks a lot."

Mushu stared blankly. "Your point is . . . ?"

The First Ancestor floated toward Mushu. "The point is—we will be sending a *real* dragon to bring Mulan back."

"But *I'm* a real dragon!" Mushu cried.

"You are not worthy of this task," the First Ancestor scoffed. "Now go—awaken the Great Stone Dragon!"

And with that, he tossed the tiny dragon out the temple door.

Mushu shuffled into the garden. So he messed up a previous assignment. So what? Anybody could make a mistake. How many centuries were they going to hold that against him? At last he reached the Great Stone Dragon. He leaned back, staring way up into the statue's stony face.

What makes *him* so special? Mushu wondered. With a sigh, he began to bang his gong. "Yo, Rocky! Wake up! You've gotta go fetch Mulan! Come on, boy. Go get her!"

But the Great Stone Dragon didn't move.

Mushu began to climb up its side. "Hello!" he shouted. Still no answer. So Mushu reared back and—*whack!* He struck the Great Stone Dragon on the ear with his gong.

Uh-oh. The ear broke off in his hand!

Mushu tried to stick the ear back on, but it was no use.

With a great shudder, the entire Great Stone Dragon crumbled to the ground!

When the dust cleared, Mushu poked his head out of the rubble. The Great Stone Dragon's stony face—the only piece left intact—stared back at him with sightless eyes.

"Oh, man!" Mushu groaned. "They're gonna kill me!"

"Great Stone Dragon! Have you awakened?"

Mushu froze. It was the voice of the First Ancestor, who gazed out the window of the temple.

Mushu did the only thing he could think of. He faked it.

He raised the face of the Great Stone Dragon above the bushes. He lowered his voice and answered, "I, ah, yes! I just woke up. I am the Great Stone Dragon. I will go forth and fetch Mulan!"

"Go!" the First Ancestor called out. "The fate of the Fa family rests in your claws."

"Don't even worry about it!" Mushu answered. "I will not lose face!" But as he said it, the weight of the stone dragon's head tipped him over backwards and he tumbled down the hill. At the bottom of the hill, the little dragon sat up, frowning. "That's great. Now what? I'm doomed. And all 'cause 'Miss Man' decided to take her little masquerade show on the road!"

Suddenly Mushu felt a tug on his tail.

He glanced down. A little cricket chirped up at him.

"What do you mean, 'Go get her'?" Mushu asked. "You crazy? The ancestors don't want me near her." He jerked his head toward the rock pile that used to be the Great Stone Dragon. "After all I've done, I'd have to make her a *hero* to get back into the temple."

He dropped his head in his hands. But then he sat up, a look of astonishment on his face. "That's it! I'll make Mulan a hero! The ancestors will forgive me, and I'll get my old job back." He threw back his head and laughed. "Ooh! I'm brilliant."

Cri-Kee the cricket hopped off toward the gate. Mushu followed. "And what makes you think *you're* coming?" he demanded.

Cri-Kee chirped.

"You're *lucky*?" Mushu laughed. "Do I look like a sucker?"

Cri-Kee chirped an answer: No, you look like a loser!

"Who's a loser?" Mushu chased the little cricket down the road.

Many miles away, horses' hooves thundered through a forest. Suddenly the lead horseman signaled the others to stop. With a wave of his hand, he sent five of his best men into the brush.

Shan-Yu, fierce leader of the Huns, jumped down from his horse. As he waited, his falcon landed on his arm.

Soon his men returned and threw two Chinese soldiers at his feet.

"Nice work, *gentlemen*," Shan-Yu growled at the frightened scouts. "You found the Hun army."

"The emperor will stop you!" one soldier bravely countered.

"Stop me?" Shan-Yu asked in mock surprise "He *invited* me." He grabbed the second soldier by his shirtfront and raised him in the air. "By building his wall, he challenged my strength. Well, I'm here to play his game." With a laugh, he threw the sweating soldier to the ground. "Go! Tell your emperor to send his strongest armies!"

The two Imperial soldiers ran off as fast as they could.

"Hmm," Shan-Yu thought, turning to his archer. "How many men does it take to deliver a message?"

The archer grinned and put an arrow to his bow. "One."

Chapter Six

Mulan paced on a hilltop in the faint light of dawn—practicing to be a man.

"Okay, Khan," she said to her horse. "How about this?" She cleared her throat and lowered her voice as deep as she could. "Excuse me, where do I sign in? Ha! I see you have a sword. I have one, too." She tried to draw it from the scabbard, but it got stuck and she dropped it.

Khan whinnied in laughter—till Mulan's shoe struck him in the head.

"Hey, I'm working on it!" Mulan cried. "It's not as easy as it looks!"

She looked down on the army camp below. "Who am I fooling? It's going to take a miracle to get me into the army."

Suddenly a towering shadow rose on the rocks nearby. A throbbing voice wailed, "Did I hear someone ask for a miracle? Let me hear you say '*Owww!*'"

"*Ahhhh!*" Mulan screeched. "A ghost!"

"Get ready, Mulan," the voice boomed. "Your serpentine salvation is at hand. For I have been sent by your ancestors to guide you through your masquerade! Because if the army finds out you're a girl, the penalty is death! But strike fear from your heart. For I will protect you."

"Who are you?" Mulan gasped.

"Who am I? I am your one and only guardian. I am the powerful, the pleasurable, the indestructible—Mushu!"

Mulan watched in excited anticipation.

Mushu jumped out from behind a rock. Mulan blinked in surprise. "My ancestors sent a little lizard to help me?"

"Dragon!" Mushu snapped.

"But you're, uh—"

"Intimidating?" Mushu suggested. "Awe-inspiring?"

"Tiny!" Mulan said.

"Of course," Mushu replied, used to such put-downs. "I'm travel-size—for your convenience. Why, if I were my real size, your *cow* there would die of fright."

Insulted, Khan tried to bite the little dragon.

Mushu glared at the horse. "Dishonor!" he flung at Mulan. "Dishonor on you and your whole family!"

"Stop!" Mulan pulled her horse away. "I'm sorry. I've never done this before. And I could use all the help I can get."

"Then you're gonna have to trust me," Mushu said. "Okay?"

Mulan nodded.

"All right, let's get this show on the road!" Mushu ordered. "Cri-Kee—get the bags!"

* * *

Soon they were all riding down the hill toward the army camp. Mushu slipped down the back of Mulan's armor so the other soldiers wouldn't see him.

Mulan squealed.

"Quiet! You'll give me away," Mushu instructed. "Now act natural."

Mulan climbed off Khan and led him into the camp. All around her soldiers stared at her. Slowly she pulled off her helmet. Would anyone be able to tell she was a girl?

"This is it!" Mushu whispered from inside her collar. "Time to show 'em your man walk! Shoulders back, chest high, feet apart—now, strut!"

Mulan tried to do all those things at once—but it only made her walk like a duck with a stomachache. "I don't think they walk like this," she whispered.

"Believe me," Mushu whispered back.

"You're blending in perfectly,"

Mulan glanced around at the men. They were a spitting, scratching, underbathed bunch.

"They're disgusting!" Mulan whispered to Mushu.

"No, they're men," Mushu whispered back. "And you're going to have to act just like them, so pay attention."

Mulan watched as one recruit bragged to some others. "This tattoo will protect me from harm."

"Really?" a recruit named Yao replied.

Wham! He punched the first recruit in the chest. His companion Ling burst out laughing. "Hope you can get your money back!"

"I don't think I can do this," Mulan told her guardian.

"It's all attitude," Mushu instructed. "Be tough, like this guy here."

Yao spit on the ground and glared at

Mulan. "What are you looking at?"

"Punch him," Mushu whispered. "It's how men say hello!"

Mulan swaggered up and smacked Yao in the back of the head.

"Whoa!" Yao growled. "I'm gonna hit you so hard, it'll make your ancestors dizzy!"

But his friend Chien-Po pulled him away.

Yao shrugged, but taunted over his shoulder: "Eh, you ain't worth my time, chicken boy."

"Chicken boy?!" Mushu popped out of Mulan's collar. "Say that to my face, you limp noodle!"

Yao turned around, his eyes burning with rage. He grabbed Mulan and threw a punch. But Mulan ducked—and the punch hit Ling. Chien-Po tried to break up the fight, but wound up in the middle of it. As Mulan tried to sneak away, the fight shoved into a line of men waiting for food. *Crash!* They knocked over a huge cauldron of rice. Rice flew everywhere!

As the men picked themselves up from the mess and directed their anger at Mulan, Chi Fu, the emperor's aide, made some notes on his tablet before striding into the general's tent.

General Li rolled open his map of China. Beside him a young officer named Shang listened closely.

"The Huns have struck here, and here, and here," the general said. "I will take the troops up toward the Tung-Shao Pass— and stop Shan-Yu before he destroys the village."

"Excellent strategy, sir," Chi Fu said.

To Shang, the general added, "You will stay and train the new recruits. When Chi Fu believes you are ready, you will join us, . . . Captain."

Shang's eyes grew wide in astonishment as the general handed him a beautiful sword. "Captain?"

Chi Fu frowned at the general's surprising announcement. "This is a big responsibility, General. Perhaps a soldier with more experience—"

"Number one in his class," the general said. "Extensive knowledge of training techniques. An impressive military lineage." General Li smiled. "I believe Li Shang will do an excellent job."

"Oh, I will!" Shang said. "I won't let you down."

"Very good then." The general picked up his helmet. "We'll toast China's victory in the Imperial City."

To Chi Fu, he said, "I expect a full report in three weeks."

The three men walked outside where the fight among the recruits was still in full force. General Li climbed upon his horse.

"Good luck, Captain." And then he rode off with his men.

"Good luck, Father," Shang whispered under his breath.

Chi Fu glowered in resentment. He was sure the young pup Shang would make a miserable mess of everything.

Don't worry, General, he thought with a sneer. I'll be sure to report on everything.

Chapter Seven

"Soldiers!" Shang shouted.

The fighting stopped as the recruits stepped back, all pointing at Mulan.

"He started it!"

"I don't need a troublemaker in my camp," Shang said sternly. "What's your name, soldier?"

"Name?" Mulan hadn't planned a name. "Uh, I've got a name," she said nervously. "And it's a *boy's* name, too. It's—Ping!"

"Let me see your papers," Shang demanded.

Mulan handed over her father's army papers. Shang's eyes widened in surprise. "Fa Zhou?" he asked. "*The* Fa Zhou?"

Chi Fu studied the small, scrawny young soldier suspiciously. "I didn't know Fa Zhou had a *son*."

Mulan prayed he didn't remember their meeting in her village. "Uh, he doesn't talk about me much," she explained.

"I can see why," Chi Fu whispered to Shang.

Shang turned to his men. "Thanks to your new friend, Ping, you'll all spend tonight picking up every single grain of rice. And tomorrow the real work begins."

All the soldiers glared at Mulan.

"You know," Mushu whispered from Mulan's collar, "I think we have to work on your people skills."

"All right, rise and shine, Sleeping Beauty!" Mushu shouted the next morning at dawn. Mulan yawned and slowly sat up.

Mushu stuffed a spoonful of porridge into her mouth. "Now, let's see your war face."

Mulan tried to look fierce.

"Ooh! I think my bunny slippers just ran for cover!" he scoffed. "Come on—scare me, girl."

Annoyed and sleepy, Mulan growled.

"All right!" Mushu praised. "Now get on out there and make me proud!"

Just then Khan stuck his head in the tent and whinnied.

"What do you mean, the troops just left!" Mushu said.

"What?" Hopping into her boots, Mulan rushed out of the tent.

Mushu ran after her. "Wait! You forgot your sword!"

When Mulan reached the training grounds, she heard Chi Fu shouting at the disorganized troops. "Order, people, order!"

"I'd like pan-fried noodles!" one soldier shouted.

"Moo goo gai pan!" another called out.

Chi Fu fumed. "That's not funny!"

As Mulan joined the group, the other soldiers began to tease her.

"Looks like Rice Boy slept in this morning," Ling smirked.

"Soldiers!" Shang shouted as he approached the group. "You will assemble swiftly and silently every morning."

"Oooh, tough guy," Yao said with a snicker.

. Shang drew his bow and fired an arrow high into a pole behind the men. "Yao—thanks for volunteering." He pointed at the pole. "Retrieve the arrow."

Grumbling, Yao bowed, then headed for the pole.

"One moment," Shang called out. "You're missing something."

He tied a disk to Yao's wrist with a colorful silk ribbon. "This represents discipline." He tied a similar disk to Yao's other wrist. "And this represents strength. You need both to reach the arrow."

With a determined scowl, Yao began to climb the pole. But the disks were too heavy, and he fell to the ground. Chien-Po, Ling, and Mulan, in turn, tried to reach the arrow with the disks tied to their wrists.

All failed.

"Did they send me daughters when I asked for sons?" Shang complained. "Somehow, I'll make a man out of every one of you."

For the next few days, Mulan worked harder than she ever had. To defeat the Huns, Shang told them, they must have the strength of a raging fire.

Late one afternoon Mulan, exhausted, collapsed on the ground.

Shang walked over and handed her Khan's reins. "You're not suited for war with the Huns. I'll never make a soldier out of you. Pack up and go home."

Mulan's heart sank. But as she turned to leave, she spotted Shang's arrow still stuck in the pole. If only she could recover that arrow, she would have succeeded in one thing.

Determined to try once more, she tied the disks to her wrists and started to climb the pole—only to fail once more.

Then she got an idea.

She tied the two stone disks together and used them as a brace to pull herself up the pole. Yao, Ling, Chien-Po, and all the other soldiers stopped to watch her in admiration as she struggled to the top.

When Mulan reached the arrow, she yanked it from the wood and held it aloft. Shang came out of his tent to see what all the commotion was about, and Mulan threw the arrow at his feet in triumph.

The soldiers cheered. Even Shang seemed impressed.

Mulan smiled. At last—she'd proved she belonged.

Chapter Eight

One night Mulan, Mushu, and Cri-Kee listened by the tent as Chi Fu berated Shang. "You think your troops are ready to fight? Ha! They wouldn't last a minute against the Huns."

"They completed their training," Shang protested.

"Those boys are no more fit to be soldiers than you are to be captain. Ha! Just wait till the general reads my report. Your troops will never see battle."

Chi Fu turned away but Shang grabbed him by the collar. "We're not finished," he said angrily.

Chi Fu glared as he removed Shang's hand. "Be careful, Captain. The general may be your father. But I'm the emperor's counsel. And by the way—I got *that* job on my own. You're dismissed," Chi Fu said with a sarcastic smirk.

Shang stormed out of the tent, disgusted.

Outside in the darkness Mulan called out to Shang. "For what it's worth, I think you're a great captain!"

Shang turned briefly, then hurried off.

"I saw that!" Mushu scolded. "You like him, don't you?"

"No!" Mulan exclaimed. "I, uh . . ."

"Uh-huh." Mushu rolled his eyes. Didn't they have enough to worry about without a complication like that? He jammed his fists on his hips. "Go to your tent!"

Then Mushu sat down to think. Chi Fu's interference with the recruit's training was a problem. He needed to get Mulan into the action—soon! Otherwise she'd never be a hero.

"Come on, Cri-Kee," he said. "It's time we took this war into our own hands."

Together they sneaked into Chi Fu's tent. With Mushu directing, Cri-Kee wrote a note and signed it "General Li."

A short while later Chi Fu burst into Shang's tent. "Captain! Urgent news from the general!" He held up the fake note that Cri-Kee had written. "We're needed at the front."

Outside Mushu grinned at Cri-Kee. "Pack your bags, Cri-Kee. We're taking this show on the road!"

As soon as they could break camp, Shang led his troops through the forest. They sang as they hiked into the mountains, still covered with the last snows of spring. Suddenly the men stopped singing. Off in the distance they saw black smoke curling into the sky. Slowly, carefully they made their way to a village. Or what was left of it. The village was in ruins, nearly burned to the ground.

"Search for survivors," Shang said solemnly.

But there were none.

Mulan walked slowly through the village. Growing up, she'd heard frightening tales of the horrible Huns.

Today, as she walked through the village, she saw that those stories were true.

Just then something on the ground caught her eye. She bent and picked it up. It was a child's doll.

Shang jumped from his horse and came toward her, his eyes filled with disbelief. "I don't understand," he said. "My father should have been here."

Then they joined Chi Fu on the bluff and looked down onto what was left of a battlefield. Shields, swords, and flags littered the snowy ground. His father had been here after all. His army had fought the Huns—and lost.

Chien-Po came forward carrying something. A helmet. "The general . . . ," he said sadly.

Shang slowly took his father's helmet, then turned away. At the top of the bluff he planted his sword in the snow. He placed his father's helmet on top, then, kneeling, bowed his head.

"I'm sorry," Mulan whispered.

After a moment of silence, he pulled himself together, curtly nodded at Mulan, and quickly mounted his horse.

"The Huns are moving quickly," he called to his men. His face was hard and cold as he pointed to the mountains. "We'll make better time to the Imperial City through the Tung-Shao Pass. We're the only hope for the emperor now. Move out!"

Mulan laid the doll beside the general's

With the help of Little Brother, Mulan cleverly feeds the chickens before racing to the matchmaker's.

Mulan is pushed and pulled, primped and polished to be presentable for the matchmaker.

Mulan hardly recognizes herself! The weight of her future and her family's honor rests on her shoulders.

Mulan will never pass as a perfect daughter.

Fa Zhou soothes Mulan's troubled heart.

"Please, sir, my father has already fought bravely for the emperor," Mulan protests.

With a flash of the blade, Mulan slices off her hair so she can fight in her father's place.

"I live!" says Mushu.

Uh-oh! The fate of Mulan and her family rests in Mushu's hands after he accidentally destroys the Great Stone Dragon.

"I don't need a troublemaker in my camp," Shang tells Mulan after she is blamed for a fight.

Shang sets a high standard.

To defeat the Huns, the soldiers must be swift and powerful.

Mulan is exhausted by the hard work she and the other soldiers must do to prepare for battle with the Huns.

At last—Mulan proves that she belongs with the other soldiers.

Mulan and her fellow soldiers are ambushed by the Huns.

Mulan notices a way out of their predicament.

Mulan rescues Shang from the avalanche.

"A life for a life," says Shang. "We leave her here."

Mulan cleverly disguises her friends as women to slip into the palace and save the Emperor.

helmet. Then she joined the others in a war that was suddenly all too real.

Weary and cold, Mulan and her fellow soldiers marched through the mountain pass. Khan pulled the munitions wagon, with Mushu and Cri-Kee perched inside.

Thunk!

An arrow struck Shang's armor and knocked him to the ground.

Mulan and the other soldiers looked up in surprise.

Huns—hundreds of them! From the mountain a downpour of flaming arrows rained on them.

A flaming arrow hit the munitions wagon. Mulan cut Khan free seconds before—

Boom! The ammunition exploded. Mulan caught Mushu and took cover with the rest of the soldiers behind an outcropping of rocks.

Their cannons roared. Hurriedly, the men started to unload their ammunition. Then the mountain fell silent. Mulan watched hopefully as the last wisps of smoke cleared. Had they defeated the Huns?

Then a Hun horseman appeared—Shan-Yu—followed by a line of soldiers that stretched as far as the eye could see. Shang turned to his men. "Prepare to fight. If we die, we die with honor. Yao, aim the last cannon at Shan-Yu."

Mulan drew her sword. But in the blade she saw the reflection of the mountain, and an idea formed in her mind.

Shink! She sheathed her sword. Grabbing the last cannon, she carried it out from behind the defensive line—toward Shan-Yu, who was galloping toward her on his horse.

"Ping!" Shang called after his soldier. "Come back!"

But Mulan ignored him. With trembling hands she pulled out the flint to light the cannon and fire the last shot.

Slam! Shan-Yu's falcon struck, knocking the flint into the snow. Mulan struggled to her knees, grabbed Mushu, and yanked his tail.

Whoosh! Flame shot out of the tiny dragon's mouth and lit the cannon's fuse.

But the shot went way over Shan-Yu's shoulder.

"How could you miss?" Mushu shrieked. "He was three feet in front of you!"

But Mulan had missed on purpose. The rocket exploded on the mountaintop. The rocks crumbled into a snowy avalanche that tumbled down the mountain. Shan-Yu saw what Mulan had done and slashed at her with his sword, but she dodged him as the avalanche buried Shan-Yu and his horde.

Mulan tried to get away, but the last wave of snow piled into her and Khan. Using his powerful hooves as leverage, Khan dug his way out of the mounds of snow, with Mulan clinging to his back. She searched the battlefield for Shang.

At last she found him half-buried in the snow. Using all her strength, she dragged his limp body onto her horse.

Safely back with his troops, Shang looked at Mulan. "Ping, you're the craziest man I've ever met—and for that I owe you my life. From now on, you have my trust."

Mulan smiled, delighted by her captain's praise.

"Let's hear it for Ping!" Ling shouted. "The bravest of us all!" All the soldiers cheered.

But instead of pride, Mulan suddenly felt the world spin. The last words she heard before blacking out were Shang's:

"He's wounded! Get help!"

* * *

Shang and his men waited anxiously outside the medic's tent.

At last the medic came out. With a look of concern on his face, he whispered in Shang's ear. Shang was stunned by the medic's shocking news. Then he frowned and strode into the tent.

Inside, Mulan woke and smiled up into her captain's face.

But his expression was hard and cold.

Mulan gasped and touched her chest, which was covered in bandages. In treating her wound, the doctor had discovered her secret.

"I can explain—," she began.

But then Chi Fu burst into the tent. "So it's true!" he cried, disgusted. "I knew there was something wrong with you!" Roughly he dragged her from the tent and announced to all the soldiers, "She's a woman! Treacherous swine!"

He threw her to the ground.

The soldiers gaped at her in disbelief.

Mulan looked up into the startled faces of her friends—Yao, Ling, and Chien-Po. "My name is Mulan," she said quietly. Her eyes turned to Shang, begging him to understand. "I did it to save my father."

"High treason!" Chi Fu nearly shrieked. "Ultimate dishonor!" He glared at the captain, challenging him to take action.

Shang gazed down at Mulan lying defenseless on the ground. Here was a good soldier whose quick thinking and bravery had defeated the Huns. And who had saved Shang's life.

But here was also a soldier who had lied to him—lied to them all. And who had broken the law.

Slowly Shang walked to Khan and removed Mulan's sword. As he strode back toward Mulan, her friends—Yao, Ling, and Chien-Po—stepped forward to protect her.

Chi Fu's eyes dared them to interfere. "You know the law."

Mulan trembled. She, too, knew what her punishment must be.

Shang raised the sword.

The law said Mulan must die.

Chapter Nine

Thunk! Shang threw the sword deep into the snow inches in front of Mulan.

"A life for a life," Shang said coldly. "My debt is repaid." Without another word, he mounted his horse, then called to his troops, "Move out!"

Chi Fu could not believe his eyes. "But you can't just—"

"I said move out," Shang repeated.

Later that afternoon Mulan, Mushu, and Cri-Kee huddled by a small campfire.

"I should never have left home," Mulan muttered.

"Hey, come on," Mushu said, trying to

make her feel better. "You went out to save your father's life. Who knew you'd end up disgracing your ancestors and losing all your friends?"

"Maybe I didn't do it for my father," Mulan said. "Maybe what I really wanted was to prove I could do things right. So when I looked in the mirror, I'd see someone worthwhile."

Mulan stared at her reflection in her helmet and sadly shook her head. "But I was wrong. I see nothing." Blinking back tears, she let the helmet tumble to the ground.

Touched by her sadness, Mushu picked up the helmet and spit on it, then gave it a vigorous rub. "Well, that's just 'cause this needs a little spit, that's all. Let me shine this up for you. Here, look at you. You look so pretty."

But Mulan wouldn't even look. "I'm sorry I wasted your time, Mushu. I know you tried."

Then Mushu looked at his own pitiful reflection. And he knew he had to confess.

"Look, the truth is, we're *both* frauds—fakes," he admitted. "The ancestors never sent me. They don't even *like* me! You risked your life to help people you love. I risked your life to help myself. At least you had good intentions."

Cri-Kee chirped sadly.

"Whaddya mean, you're *not* lucky?" Mushu exclaimed. "You lied to me?!" He shook his head and glared at Khan. "So what are you?" he asked the horse. "A sheep?"

"I'll have to face my father sooner or later," Mulan said at last. "Let's go home."

Mushu sighed. "Yep, this ain't gonna be pretty. But don't worry, okay? We started this together, and that's how we'll finish it. I promise." And then the feisty little dragon did something surprising. He gave Mulan a hug.

Together they packed up their few belongings.

Suddenly they heard a bloodcurdling howl from down below. Mulan, Mushu, and Cri-Kee crept to the edge of the canyon and looked down at the battlefield.

Shan-Yu! He was alive! They watched in horror as a handful of his men dug themselves out from under the snow.

Mushu whistled. "Oh no, from your freezer to your front door in minutes."

The Huns turned toward the distant lights of the Imperial City, home of the emperor. Where Shang was headed.

Mulan grabbed up her sword and leaped onto Khan's back.

Mushu followed. He was eager to get away from the Huns, too. Only . . . she was going the wrong way!

"Uhh," he called to Mulan, "home is *that* way."

"I have to do something," Mulan

insisted. Then she headed toward the Imperial City.

Cri-Kee made a face at Mushu and followed Mulan.

Mushu rolled his eyes. The girl was determined! But what could he do? He'd promised to stick with her. "Eeee-ha-a!" he cried enthusiastically and hurried after her.

Dusk enveloped the Imperial City. At this time of night, Mulan's village back home would be dark and deserted. But in the Imperial City, lights flickered everywhere, and crowds of people still filled the streets. Everyone was celebrating the victory over the Huns.

Mulan rode up on her horse, frantically searching the crowd.

Then she heard an official's voice shouting across the crowd. "Make way for the heroes of China!"

Shang rode by on his horse, followed by

76

Yao, Ling, Chien-Po, and the rest of the men.

"Shang!" Mulan called out.

Shang and her friends stared at her in surprise.

"The Huns are alive!" she called. "They're in the city!"

"What?" Shang shook his head, his eyes cold and hard. "You don't belong here, Mulan. Go home."

"But, Shang!" Mulan cried. "I saw them in the mountains. I wouldn't lie about this."

"Why should I believe you?" he replied.

"Why else would I come back?" she argued. "You said you'd trust *Ping*. Why is *Mulan* any different?"

Shang had no answer for that.

Mulan warned her soldier friends, "Keep your eyes open. I know they're here." With a shout of "Hee-yaa!" she galloped off and was lost in the crowd.

At the end of the broad boulevard, the palace drums pounded. Fireworks exploded in the black sky. The emperor came out to greet Shang and his soldiers.

Down on the street Mulan had jumped off Khan and now searched the crowd for someone who would believe her. "Sir! The emperor is in danger!"

The man pushed her away and turned his back.

"But the Huns are here," she said to another man. "You have to help."

Frustrated, Mulan turned to Mushu. "They won't listen."

"You're a girl again," Mushu said with a shrug. "What do you expect?"

Then she saw Shang climb to the platform to present the emperor with Shan-Yu's sword.

"My children," the emperor called to his people. "Heaven smiles down upon the kingdom! China will sleep safely tonight!

Thanks to our brave warriors, the Huns have been defeated!" The crowd cheered. Holding Shan-Yu's sword in front of him, Shang knelt before the emperor. "I know what this means to you, Captain Li," the Emperor said gently. "Your father would have been proud."

But as Shang held out Shan-Yu's sword, a falcon swooped down from the sky and grabbed it. It soared to the palace rooftop and dropped it—into the hands of a statue.

No—not a statue. Shan-Yu! The Hun leader shook his sword over his head in an arrogant cry of victory.

Shan-Yu's men cut their way out of a parade dragon on the palace steps. Before the eyes of the stunned crowd, they knocked Shang down, grabbed the emperor, and dragged him inside the palace.

By the time Shang and his men could react, the Huns had slammed and locked the palace door.

Quickly, Mulan's soldier friends knocked over a stone statue and began to use it as a battering ram.

Mulan shook her head. "They'll never get in that way." She ran over and whistled. "Hey, guys. I've got an idea!"

Chien-Po, Ling, and Yao didn't think twice. They ran to Mulan's side. But Shang held back. Even now, it was still hard for him to trust this young woman who had deceived him.

Mulan couldn't wait for him to make up his mind about her. If they were going to save the emperor, they had to act—now!

Mulan prepared the soldiers for battle, but she did it in a clever way—makeup, bracelets, wigs, and dresses. She dressed them up like women!

Mulan knew the Huns would be watching for soldiers. She figured they wouldn't pay much attention to women inside the palace.

Then she felt a tap on her shoulder. She turned around.

It was Shang!

Mulan smiled—they could face anything now. Quickly she, Yao, Ling, and Chien-Po used their sashes to climb the columns—just as she'd climbed the pole to fetch Shang's arrow during training. Shang followed, using his cape.

Once inside they slipped along the halls.

"We're almost there," Mulan said. "Any questions?"

"Yeah," Yao said. "Does this dress make me look fat?"

Chapter Ten

On a palace balcony, Shan-Yu sneered at the emperor. "How disappointing," he drawled. "These people *fear* you?"

The emperor replied with dignity, "They *respect* me."

Shan-Yu clucked his tongue. "Fools. Now that we have their attention, bow down." Shan-Yu raised his gleaming sword above the emperor. "I'll make this quick."

The emperor did not move.

"Your walls have fallen," Shan-Yu cried angrily. "And so have you. Bow to me!"

But the emperor would not bend. "Now matter how the wind howls, a mountain cannot bow to it."

Shan-Yu's face turned red with rage. "Then you will kneel—in pieces." He raised his sword.

But as he brought it down—*clang!*

Shang blocked the blow with his own. As he wrestled the Hun to the ground, Mulan and her friends ran onto the balcony. Mulan threw a piece of cloth over a banner hanging from a pillar. Chien-Po scooped up the emperor in his arms. "Uh, sorry, Your Majesty," he whispered.

Then they used the banner as a zip-line and slid the emperor safely down to the ground. Ling and Yao quickly followed.

"Noooo!" With a cry of rage, Shan-Yu shook Shang off, knocking him unconscious. He ran to the edge of the balcony and saw that the emperor had escaped safely to the ground. Shan-Yu let out a roar of frustration. Then he grabbed the groggy Shang and held his sword to Shang's throat. "*You* took away my victory."

Suddenly—*thunk!*—something soft hit the Hun in the back of the head. He whirled around.

Mulan had thrown her shoe at him. "No, *I* did."

Shan-Yu stared in recognition. "You're the soldier from the mountains!" He grabbed up his sword and began to chase her.

Mulan ran. She ran out onto the roof just as Shan-Yu caught up with her. She looked around for a weapon, but could only find her fan. With a snap of her wrist, she opened the fan and gazed over it at the Hun.

Shan-Yu threw back his head and laughed. "It looks like you're out of ideas." He stabbed his sword through the painted silk of her fan.

"Not quite," she answered. She snapped the fan closed on the blade, then twisted his sword from his hand. "Ready, Mushu?" she hollered.

Shan-Yu whirled around. Mushu rode in on a black kite. When he ripped off the wings, they could see he had a rocket strapped to his back.

"Ready, baby!" Mushu shouted with glee. With a quick blast of fire from his mouth, he lit a small stick and handed it to Cri-Kee. "Light me!"

The little cricket lit the rocket's fuse.

The rocket took off toward Mulan and Shan-Yu.

Mulan stabbed the sword through Shan-Yu's tunic, pinning him to the roof. Then she vaulted out of the way.

The rocket smashed into Shan-Yu. Mushu clung to the sword as the rocket carried Shan-Yu off the roof toward the fire-works tower.

Grabbing Mushu and Cri-Kee, Mulan broke into a run. "Get off the roof! Get off the roof!" she shouted.

As Shan-Yu and the rocket slammed into

the fireworks tower, a towering massive fireball erupted.

Shang staggered out of the palace—just as it blew up behind him.

He looked back over his shoulder as building fragments rained down around him.

Chapter Eleven

Fireworks showered the night sky as the palace blew up.

Seconds later Mulan flew through the air and landed on Shang, knocking him down the palace steps. Mulan hugged him in relief.

A second later Shan-Yu's sword fell at their feet with a clang!

Then Mushu and Cri-Kee dropped from the sky.

Shang smiled as he saw Yao, Ling, and Chien-Po emerge unharmed.

Then Chi Fu stumbled from the wreckage, his hat smoldering. "Where is she?" he shrieked. "Now she's done it! What a *mess!*"

And then he saw her. That disgraceful, deceitful *female*! In a rage, he stumbled toward her.

But Mulan's friends formed a circle around her.

"Stand aside!" Chi Fu shouted. "That creature's not worth protecting."

"She's a hero!" Shang protested.

"She's a *woman*!" Chi-Fu spluttered. "She'll *never* be worth *anything*!"

Shang grabbed him by the neck of his tunic. "Listen, you pompous—"

"*That*," said a stern voice, "is enough!"

Everyone turned.

The emperor!

"Your Majesty," Shang said with a bow, "I can explain—"

But the emperor held up his hand and waved the men aside as his eyes fell upon Mulan. Nervously she bowed her head.

"I've heard a great deal about you, Fa Mulan," he said sternly. "You stole your father's armor. You ran away from home. Pretended to be a soldier. Lied to your commanding officer. Dishonored the Chinese Army. *Destroyed* my palace. . . ."

Mulan lowered her eyes, trembling in fear.

"And," the emperor said more gently, "you have saved us all."

Mulan looked up in surprise. The emperor was smiling—at her! And then he did something that emperors do not do.

He bowed to her.

Mulan watched in astonishment as everyone in the entire plaza followed his example. Just a few days earlier, she had been labeled by the matchmaker as one who would never bring honor to her family.

And now an entire city had bowed in her honor.

"Chi Fu!" the emperor called.

Chi Fu stepped forward. "Yes, Your Excellency?"

"See that this woman is made a member of my council."

Chi Fu nearly choked. "A member—what?" Impossible! he thought to himself. Unheard of! "Ah . . . there are no council positions open, Your Majesty." There, that should take care of that!

"Very well," the emperor said. He turned to Mulan. "Then you can have *his* job."

Chi Fu fainted.

Mulan gazed into the eyes of the emperor. No woman in the history of China had ever served on the emperor's council. But she knew where she longed to be. "With all due respect, Your Excellency, I think I've been away from home long enough."

The emperor smiled as if he understood. "Then take this," he said. He removed the royal crest that hung around his neck and slipped it on over her head. "So your family will know what you have done for me.

"And this"—the emperor gave her Shan-Yu's sword—"so the world will know what you have done for China."

Mulan accepted the gifts reverently. And then—unable to stop herself—she threw her arms around the emperor's neck.

"Is she allowed to do that?" Yao whispered to Ling.

Perhaps it was not the most dignified thing to do. But it was the only way to express the joy in her heart. The emperor looked pleasantly surprised.

Then Chien-Po gathered up Mulan, Yao, and Ling in his arms and they shared a group embrace.

Mulan shyly turned to Shang.

They looked at each other in awkward silence.

"Um, you're a—" Shang struggled with the words. At last he simply said, "You fight good." And he shook her hand.

"Oh," Mulan said, trying to hide her

disappointment. But what else had she expected him to say? "Thank you."

Then she climbed onto her horse, with Mushu and Cri-Kee. "Khan, let's go home."

Shang watched her ride off, wanting somehow to stop her.

Beside him, the emperor cleared his throat. "The flower that blooms in adversity is the most rare and beautiful of all."

"Sir?" Shang asked, a puzzled look on his face.

The emperor shook his head. He tried again: "You don't meet a girl like that every dynasty."

As Shang gazed into the distance thoughtfully, the emperor remembered what he had said to his court not so long ago: "A single grain of rice can tip the scale. One man may be the difference between victory and defeat."

How true, he thought with a smile. Or one very special young woman!

The morning stars were fading in the blush of sunrise as Mulan reached home at last. She smiled when she saw her father already up and sitting beneath a tree.

A soft breeze blew through the garden, and a blossom from the tree floated into Fa Zhou's lap. He picked it up and gazed at it tenderly.

And then he looked up to see his daughter. She was home!

But before he could rise to his feet, Mulan knelt before him. She laid a sword in his lap. "I brought you the sword of Shan-Yu," she said. "And the crest of the emperor. They're gifts—to honor the Fa family."

Fa Zhou accepted the gifts solemnly, but he immediately set them aside and gathered Mulan into his arms. "The greatest gift and honor," he said with tears of joy in his eyes, "is having you for a daughter. I've missed you so."

"I've missed you, too, Ba-Ba."

At last—she had brought honor to her family. And best of all, she'd done it her own way.

"Isn't it wonderful?" Fa Li said, watching from the house.

Grandmother Fa shrugged. "She brings home a sword? If you ask me, she should have brought home a man."

"Excuse me."

Mulan's mother and grandmother turned to find a handsome young man waiting nervously at their gate. "Does Fa Mulan live here?"

Mother and Grandmother exchanged a look, then pointed to the garden.

Shang hurried toward the garden. "Honorable Fa Zhou . . . ," he began with a deep bow. Then he saw Mulan. "Uh . . . Mulan . . . ," he stammered, "you forgot your helmet . . . I mean," he continued, turning to Fa Zhou, "actually *your* helmet . . . that she stole . . . uh . . ."

Mulan and her father looked at each other. Then Fa Zhou motioned to Shang, stepping away to let the two talk.

"Besides, it would be a shame to lose a good helmet . . ." Shang was still having trouble saying what he meant.

Mulan laughed. "Would you like to stay for dinner?"

"Would you like to stay forever?" Grandmother Fa called out.

"Well, come on," Mushu said to the First Ancestor as they watched from the temple. "Who did a good job?"

"Oh, all right," the First Ancestor admitted, crossing his arms. Then he muttered under his breath, "You can be a guardian again."

Mushu gasped. "Whaaat?"

The First Ancestor threw up his hands. "I said," he repeated irritably, "you can be a guardian again."

"Waaaaaaahhh!!!" Mushu squealed.

Cri-Kee banged the gong again and again and woke up the other guardians.

All night long they celebrated their good fortune.

Generation after generation would tell of Mulan's courage and devotion. And her story would bring honor to herself and her family forever.